Published by Renegade Arts Canmore Ltd trading as Renegade Arts Entertainment Ltd
Office of publication: 25 Prospect Heights, Canmore, Alberta T1W 2S2 Canada
The characters and events depicted in this book are fictional.
Any similarity between the fictional characters to actual persons whether living or dead is completely unintentional.

Renegade Arts Entertainment is
Alexander Finbow Alan Grant Doug Bradley
John Finbow Nick Wilson and Jennifer Taylor.

First Printing 2015

Written by Mandi Kujawa
Illustrated by Claude St. Aubin
Lettering by Annie Parkhouse
Editor and publisher Alexander Finbow

Printed in Canada by Friesens

www.renegadeartsentertainment.com

ISBN: 9780992150877

Always find a time and a place for what you love.

ENVIRONMENTAL BENEFITS STATEMENT

Renegade Arts Canmore Ltd saved the following resources by printing the pages of this book on chlorine free paper made with 10% post-consumer waste.

TREES	WATER	SOLID WASTE	GREENHOUSE GASES
1	516	34	95
FULLY GROWN	GALLONS	POUNDS	POUNDS

 Environmental impact estimates were made using the Environmental Paper Network Paper Calculator 3.2. For more information visit www.papercalculator.org.

MIX
Paper from responsible sources
FSC® C016245
www.fsc.org

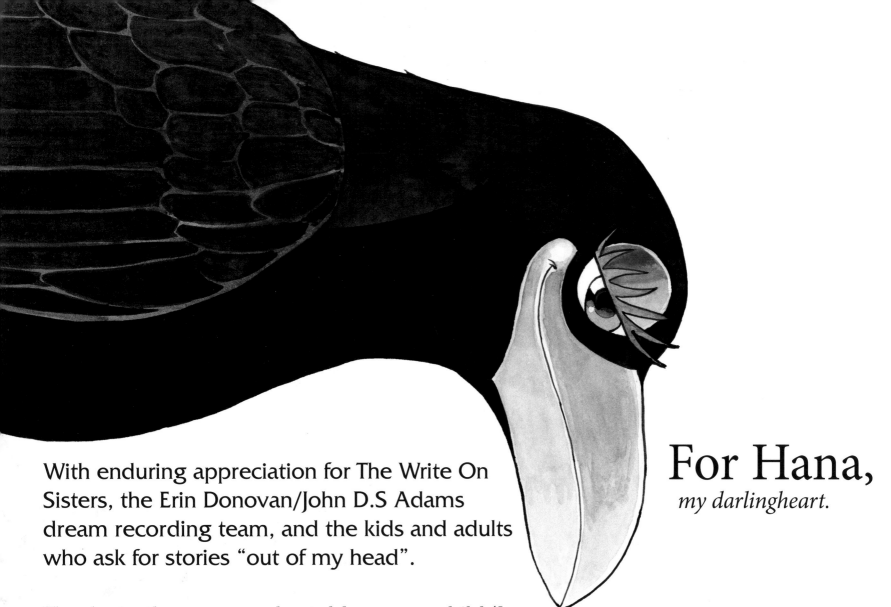

With enduring appreciation for The Write On Sisters, the Erin Donovan/John D.S Adams dream recording team, and the kids and adults who ask for stories "out of my head".

Thanks to the person who told me as a child 'I hope you don't think you're singing in tune..." You gave me the idea for my story!

The following singing/storytelling coaches helped rehabilitate me. Richard Armstrong, Marguerite Witvoet, and Jay O'Callahan.

For Hana,
my darlingheart.

A great BIG thanks to Alexander Finbow for hearing this being told and deciding to make it into a book!

Claude St. Aubin - you are a gift.

JACQUELINE THE SINGING CROW

By Mandi Kujawa

Illustrated by Claude St-Aubin

One morning Jacqueline and her feathered friends were high atop of a tall pine tree.

Way down below them was a little park with picnic tables and benches.

All around the little park was a little town.

And all around the little town was a huge forest stretching in all directions.

Jacqueline spotted a hairy caterpillar on a bush near a family picnicking in the park below. Gracefully she flew down and landed on the bush. She was just about to eat the caterpillar when she became aware of voices.

Human voices.

Jacqueline was stunned.

She lost her appetite and couldn't go back to her friends in the pine tree.
She had to get away to think about this.

She flew deep into the forest and landed on a branch. She looked herself over.
Well, she didn't have *red* feathers like a robin, or *blue* feathers like a blue jay.
She didn't even have a yellow beak like a duck.

But it was a wonderful, glorious, marvelous day and a squirrel dashing about caught her attention.

Chitter, chatter, chitter, chatter.

Stop. Start. Stop. Start. Leap! It's hard to stay in a bad mood when you're really looking at a squirrel.

Jacqueline felt so much better that she was about to fly back to her flock when she heard voices.

Human voices.

She tucked herself in tight to the trunk of the tree to hide...

...but it was no use because the humans down below were birdwatchers.

Can't... even... sing?

Jacqueline sang all the time. She sang with her friends, she sang with her family, she sang for her joy! And to find out now that people thought she sounded *horrible*... It was too much!

Disgusting, boring, can't even sing.

She had to get away. Far, far away where she would never, ever be near human beings again.

She launched herself into the air
and flew... south. Now, if she'd
flown north she might have had
her wish, there are a lot fewer
humans in the north of Canada.

But she flew south right out of Canada...

and through the

United States...   and beyond Mexico.

Farther and farther south she flew, over days and weeks,

until at last she found herself in the middle of a vast rainforest.

It was warm, the air was sweet. Exotic flowers bloomed and ripe fruits hung heavy on the branches. Everywhere she looked there were tasty looking tropical bugs and there were no humans in sight.

But Jacqueline had never felt more miserable in all her life.

Here she was with her drab, boring feathers and there were birds here with *beaks* more colourful than a rainbow. Birds with dazzling feathers in every jeweled colour, and birds with sweet songs.

But she had nowhere else to go,

and she was too tired to fly any further.

Three days later, Jacqueline woke up feeling fabulously well-rested, and without thinking, started to sing

Jacqueline stopped and looked around in a panic...

...but none of the pretty birds seemed to mind her singing.

They sang, and she sang!

She sang in the mornings, she sang in the afternoons, and she sang in the evenings.
Happy months passed.

Then one day Jacqueline woke up and found herself missing singing along with her friends and her family in the old pine tree.

But her thoughts of home were interrupted by voices.

Human voices!

She hid among the lush leaves, but it was no use. The people down below were... birdwatchers.

Señora Entusiasta looked through her spotting scope and said to her companion...

FLASH!
FLASH!
FLASH!

Jacqueline posed

FLASH!
FLASH!
FLASH!

while the humans took
photo after photo.

FLASH! FLASH!

When the light faded the two bird watchers agreed they'd be back the very next day with all their bird-watching friends!

But the next day, Jacqueline was not there. She had decided to fly home.

Back in Canada and back in the top of the tall pine tree, her friends and family greeted her,

"CAW! CAW! CAW!!"

which roughly translates as: "Jacqueline, where've you been?!"

"What were you *thinking*?!"

So Jacqueline told them where she'd been and what she'd been thinking.

Partway through her story, one of the crows noticed a large grasshopper down below.

I'll be right back. Just grabbing a snack.

Down he flew, only to be met with shouts from a nearby human,

Then without worrying
at all, Jacqueline opened
her beak and sang.

She sang for her friends,
she sang for her family.

She sang for herself.

Jacqueline

Mandi Kujawa

Mandi Kujawa (pronounced coo-yah-va) Mandi lives in the mountain town of Banff, Alberta. She is a storyteller/singer/musician who delights in sharing words and music with kids, teens, and adult audiences. Mandi is thrilled to add Claude St Aubin's artwork to the mix!

Claude St. Aubin lives in small town Raymond, Alberta. He has worked as an artist on many comic books including CAPTAIN CANUCK, THE GREEN LANTERN, X FILES, R.E.B.E.L.S, and THE LOXLEYS AND THE WAR OF 1812.

Photo by Hana Kujawa

Photo by Jacqueline St. Aubin

Look out for more great books from Renegade Arts Entertainment, including:

THE LOXLEYS AND THE WAR OF 1812

Written by Alan Grant & Mark Zuehlke
Illustrated by Claude St. Aubin and Lovern Kindzierski

This award winning graphic novel features 101 page historically accurate comic strip about a Canadian family caught up in the war, and an illustrated summary of the war and its implications for Canada and America written by acclaimed Canadian military historian Mark Zuehlke, also includes maps and illustrations.

"An example of graphic novel storytelling at its best." author Dwight Jon Zimmerman.

THE LOXLEYS AND CONFEDERATION

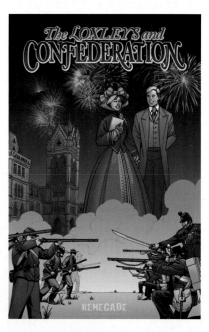

Written by Mark Zuehlke, Alexander Finbow, and Niigaanwewidam James Sinclair
Illustrated by Claude St. Aubin and Chris Chuckry

It is 1864 and threats from America once again place the Canadas in grave danger. The story of the birth of Canada is told as a travelogue as George Loxley reports on the attempts to bring the provinces together, joined by his daughter, and granddaughter Lilian. It is Lilian's diary entries and her developing love story that threads the history together.

For more information on our books, visit our website:

www.RenegadeArtsEntertainment.com